MULCH-POWERED
ROCKET BOOSTER

DINNER-MATIC

OUT OF
STOCK

ENGINE
ROOM

ESCAPE
POD

STATUS:
EMPTY

LARDER

MEDICAL BAY

WATER TANK

STOW AWAYS

For Nora, Toby and my
hoard of siblings better known
as Joe, Paul, Tonia and Tim.

SUPER STEALTH COVERT CRUISER

FOREST FLEET 704

First published in 2014 by Nosy Crow Ltd. The Crow's Nest, 10a Lant Street, London SE1 1QR

www.nosycrow.com

ISBN 978 0 85763 322 4

Nosy Crow and associated logos are trademarks and /or registered trademarks of Nosy Crow Ltd.

Text and illustration © Elys Dolan 2014

The right of Elys Dolan to be identified as the author and illustrator of this work has been asserted.

A CIP catalogue record for this book is available from the British Library.

Printed in China

1 3 5 7 9 8 6 4 2

NUTS
IN
SPACE

BY ELYS DOLAN

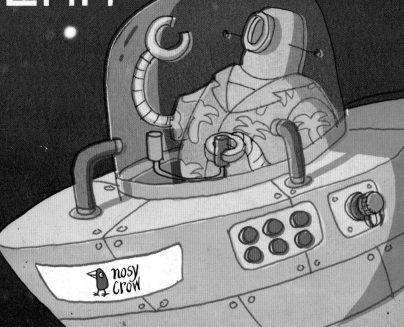

It is written that at the very edge of deep space,
there can be found The Lost Nuts of Legend.
The bearer of this mythical snack will be immortal,
invincible and never will it be past their bedtime. BUT . . .

The Lost Nuts of Legend must never, EVER be eaten.

The crew of the Forest Fleet's finest Starship, a team

carefully chosen to find the Nuts for the good of all

creaturekind, are now returning from their mission

triumphant, with the Nuts on board. The journey has been

long and hard, and now there is no food left. Everyone's

hungry and a bit grumpy. Luckily, all they have to do now is . . .

. . . GO HOME!

That's different.

Oh look, floating words.

How will we get home now?!

And what will we do with The Lost Nuts of Legend?!

AAAAAAHHHH!!!!
But we're all SO hungry!!

EAT AT JIM'S

Wait! Don't panic. We'll ask for directions at the Space Station Cafe. Remember, Nut Safety is our primary concern, so pack up The Lost Nuts of Legend and get moving!

Can I just hold one?

NO.

The Starship soon arrives at the small moon but it turns out the locals aren't too keen on nuts.

NUT-FREE PLANET

SUPER STEALTH COVERT CRUISER

FOREST FLEET 704

My eye is itching!

The crew do as the Little Green Men suggest and go to ask at the forest planet down the road. The residents seem just delightful . . .

... but the bears obviously don't know The Way Home and, actually, they aren't that friendly so the crew go to look elsewhere.

Even though *some* people aren't too keen, the Starship docks at the Death Banana to ask for directions.

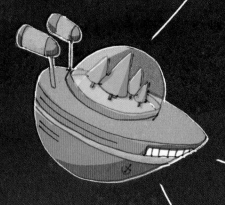

This looks like a helpful kind of place. We'll park up and ask whoever's inside.

I've got a bad feeling about this.

You're never any fun, Duck.

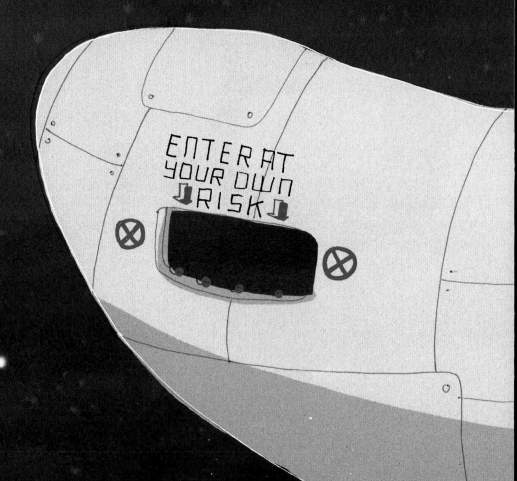

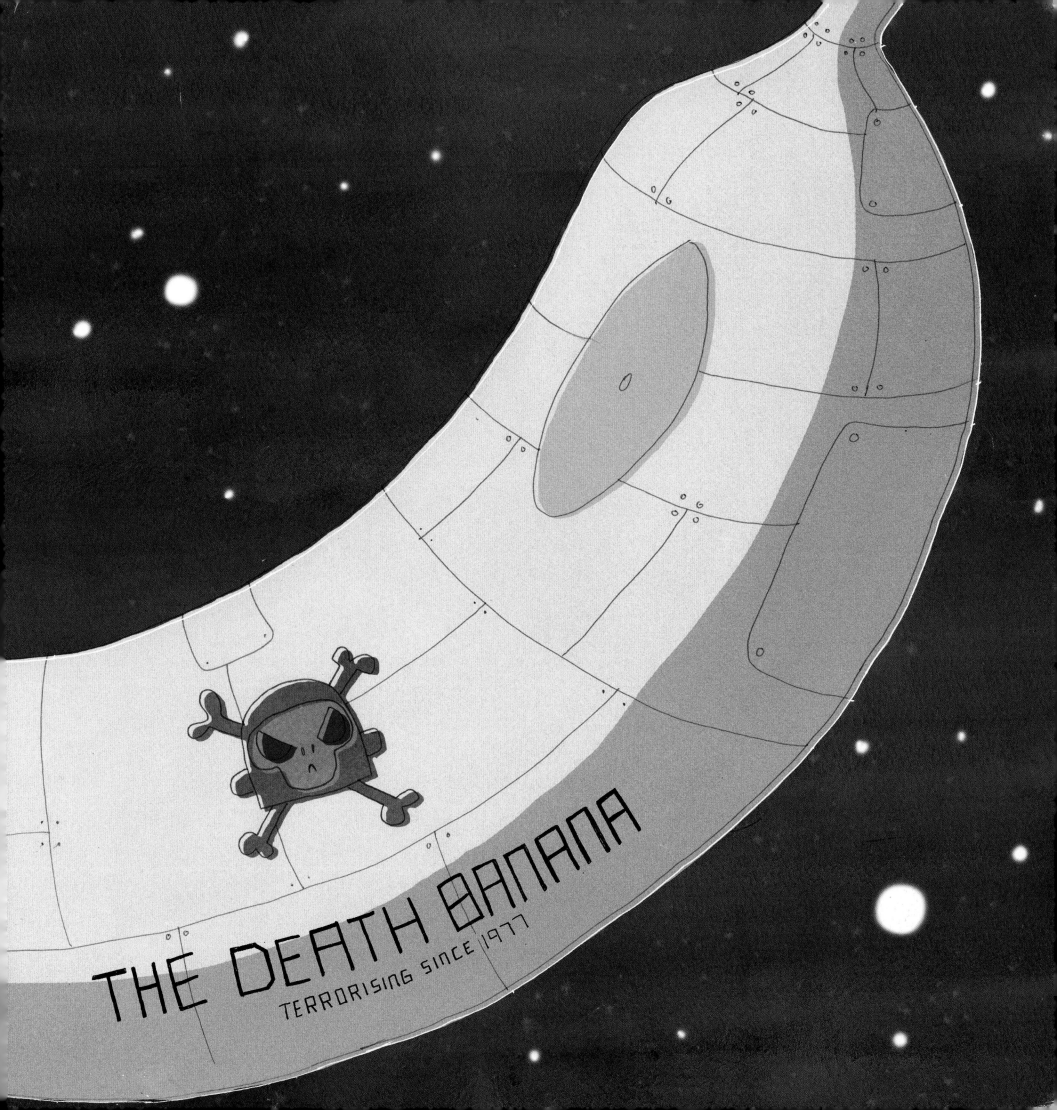

However, it turns out the monkeys are VERY interested in The Lost Nuts of Legend, so the crew make a hasty exit . . .

And so, with The Lost Nuts of Legend gone, our crew is left with only one choice — to turn the ship around and set off once again in search of more . . .

BADGER: SECURITY

DUCK MD: MEDICAL

OWL: CHIEF NAVIGATOR

FOX: POULTRY OFFICER

SQUIRREL: NUT EXPERT

BEAVER: ENGINEER

COMMANDER MOOSE

NUT STORE

ATMOSPHERE TREES

BRIDGE

SLEEPING QUARTERS

OPERATION: GATHER NUTS

LIBRARY AND LOUNGE